Colin McNaughton

We're Off to Look for ALIENS

WALKER BOOKS
AND SUBSIDIARIES
LONDON · BOSTON · SYDNEY · AUCKLAND

"Ah-ha!" said Dad.
"My alien book. Thank you,
Mister Postman."

It was Dad's new book, fresh from the printer. Dad writes children's books. He also does the pictures. He says it's hard work – although he seems to spend an awful lot of time messing about.

"Tell me what you think,"
said Dad, handing us the book.
"I hope you like it."

Dad said he was too nervous
to watch us read, so he took
the dog for a walk.

This is what we read

"Well," said Dad, back from his walk,
  "what do you think of my alien book?"
"It's brilliant, Dad," said my
  brother. "But there's a problem."
"What sort of problem?" frowned Dad.
"Well," said Mum carefully. "It's a
  great book and kids will love the pictures,

but … it's the story."
"What's wrong with it?" said Dad.
"It's a wonderful story!"
"Yes, Dad," I said. "We agree.
It's just that children like
fairy tales and stuff, and
we were wondering, Dad …